March

MW00904633

Amy L. Bursard

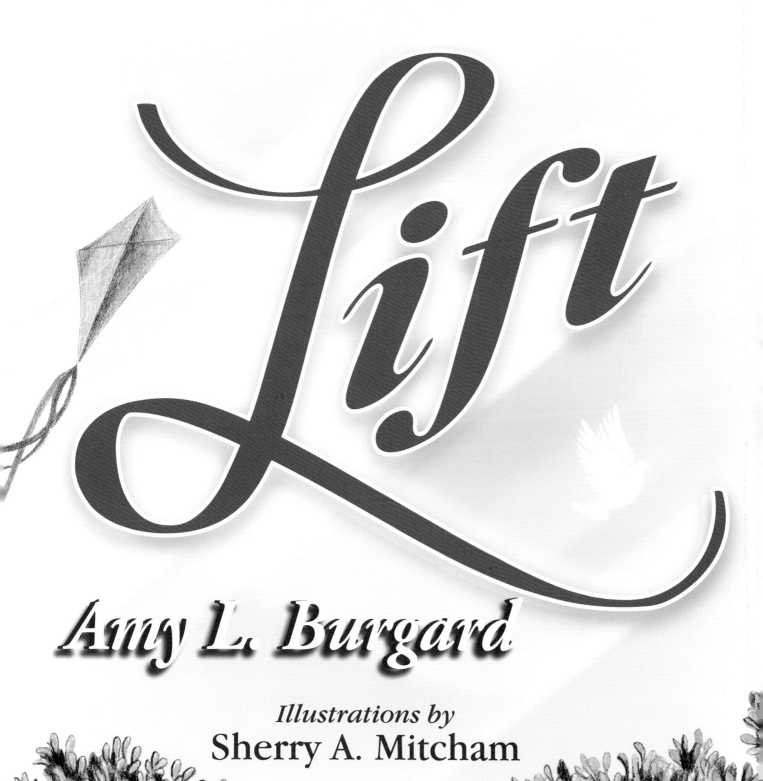

Lift

Amy L. Burgard

Illustrations by
Sherry A. Mitcham

Contact Info for Workshop Information and Comments:

www.mendingwings2fly.com

Amy L. Burgard
mendingwings2fly@gmail.com

Dedication

I dedicate this book to all of God's children
who have had to walk through
the darkness of bullying.

I truly pray this book will impact
our hearts powerfully so we will live in a world
filled with much more love and a lot less hate.

I also dedicate this book to
Mr. Gaskill
my Vice-Principal at Sanford Elementary.
He stood up for me in 4th grade and
I know it greatly impacted my life in a positive way.
The ripple effects continue to this day.

*T*oday was the big 4th of July picnic for ambassadors and their families at Parkview Park in Washington D.C. Samuel, Caleb, Victoria, and Isabella quickly became friends while playing on the swings. During their conversation, they realized they were all the same age and going to be attending the same elementary school. They had all moved during the summer from four different countries and continents. They were looking forward to starting fourth grade this year in America.

My name is Victoria. My Dad is the ambassador from England. I love riding horses. I do not have any brothers or sisters. This is my second international move in the last few years.

My name is Samuel. I love science and building rockets. I have an older sister. My dad is the ambassador from the Philippines.

My name is Isabella. I collect butterflies. My mom just gave me a porcelian figurine of one of my favorite butterflies. She is the ambassador from Argentina. I have a little brother.

My name is Caleb, I love playing soccer and I really miss my team back in my country of Ethiopia. I want to win the World Cup one day. My Dad is the ambassador from my country. I have an older brother and a younger sister.

They were glad that they were not going to be alone starting their new school year. They also realized they lived along the same row of houses.

Several weeks later, the bus arrived promptly at 7:30 in the morning. On the first day of school Samuel, Caleb, Victoria, and Isabella were excited to find out they were all in Ms. Smart's class.

Recess arrived and they were excited to be able to play on the new playground. Unfortunately they were confronted with a group of boys and girls that were waiting for them outside.

One by one the mean boys and girls made fun of them for the way they looked, spoke, and the way they dressed. They said things like "You talk funny!"

"You dress weird!"

"Do you really think you are so special because your parents are ambassadors!"

*T*hey taunted Victoria. "Shall we bow for your majesty?"

They made fun of Samuel by using their fingers to pull their eyes to look like Samuel's eyes.

The boys and girls danced around Caleb. "Show us your African tribal dance!"

A couple of kids pretended to shake maracas while performing like a spanish band in front of Isabella.

Samuel, Caleb, Victoria, and Isabella were terrified and very upset. Their excitement over their new school quickly turned into pain and disappointment.

They finally came home from the very long and tiring day. They gathered on Victoria's porch. Samuel was stewing while he thought long and hard about each face that had taunted him and his friends.

Caleb was pacing back and forth filled with anger. His peers had made fun of a tradition he and his family cherished as part of his heritage and culture.

Victoria was filled with sadness. She longed to be with her friends back in England. Isabella kept talking about how she didn't like the way she looked and how she should have worn a different outfit. She had told her mom she wanted a different hairstyle and she felt her clothes were too bright in color.

Suddenly, a dove flew down from the sky and landed on Caleb's shoulder. The dove began to fly off and Caleb started chasing after it. It landed on a nearby fountain.

At the base of the fountain something was sticking out of the grass. Caleb bent down to pick it up. It was a music box in the shape of a heart. He opened the box and it began to play *Jesus Loves Me*. Inside he found a folded piece of paper with a huge "L" on one side and on the other side it had a note.

Dear Caleb,

You are loved very much!

I created you just the way you are and you are mine.

I love the way you and your family worship me through your dance! My love for you is not based on what you do or not do. I love you always and forever.

I am asking you to love those who hurt you today. If they knew how much I loved them, they would never have treated you the way they did today.

Sing with the tune of this music box and believe the words in your heart.

I love you!
Father God

Caleb began to sing:

*Jesus loves me,
 this I know,
 for the Bible
  tells me so.
Little ones
 to Him belong,
they are weak,
 but He is strong!
Yes, Jesus loves me,
Yes, Jesus
 loves me,
Yes, Jesus
 loves me,
The Bible
 tells me so!*

So now I live with the confidence that there is nothing in the universe with the power to separate us from God's love.
– Romans 8:38a TPT

While Caleb was singing, the dove had flown back to the porch and landed on Isabella's lap. The dove flew off and she ran off to see where it was leading her. The dove landed on an object in the flower garden.

When she got up closer she saw it was a beautiful mirror. A note was attached to it with a ribbon.

She unfolded it and on one side had a huge "I".
On the other side was a personal note addressed to
Isabella.

Dear Isabella,
You are beautiful!

I love the way your hair looks and I love the beautiful colors that you wear! I made you to be you and no one else! You are my daughter and that makes you a beautiful princess.

When you believe this with your whole heart, no one and nothing can affect you the way it did today.

Remember, Isabella, that your identity is in Me and not in what others think of you. I will always accept you and love you for who you are.

Look in the mirror and repeat these words:

I am beautiful in my Father's eyes!
I am a Princess and I am treasured by the One Who made me!

I love you!
Father God

Before I formed you in
your mother's body, I chose you.
Before you were born I set you apart
to serve me. I appointed you to be a
prophet to the nations.
–Jeremiah 1:5 NIRV

The dove had now landed on Samuel's knee. Samuel was shaken out of his deep thoughts of hatred and followed the dove to see where it would take him. It landed on the lock to the back yard tool shed. Tied to the handle was an envelope with a key inside and a note. He unfolded the note and it had a huge "F" on one side and a note on the other side. It read:

Dear Samuel,
I love you!

I am so sorry you were hurt today. It was so cruel and they judged you without truly knowing you. I understand! I had the very same thing happen to Me while I walked upon the earth.

I know this is going to be difficult, but because of what I have done for you, you must do it for those boys and girls. You must forgive! I did not make you with a heart that can hold unfogiveness inside. It will only make you bitter and turn you into someone I never created you to be.

This is what I ask of you: Take this key and, as you unlock the lock, repeat after Me: I forgive each one that hurt me today. I place them into my Father's hands and I bless them in Jesus' Name.

I love you!
Father God

Samuel unlocked the lock and said the words of forgiveness. He felt the release inside of his heart from all of the bitterness he felt inside as the lock came loose and the door opened.

Put up with one another. Forgive one another if you are holding something against someone. Forgive, just as the Lord forgave you.
– Colossians 3:13 NIRV

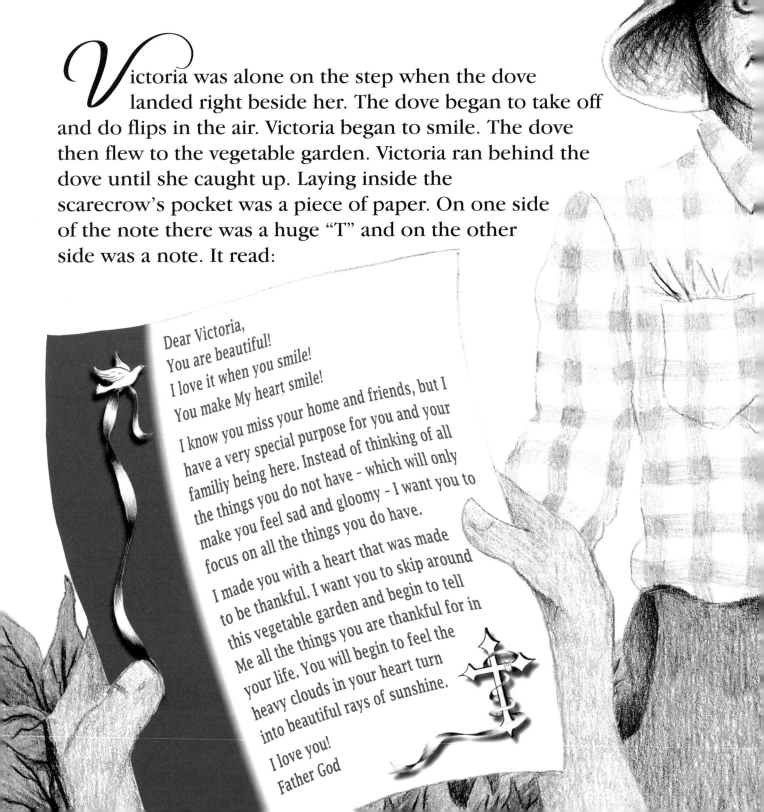

*V*ictoria was alone on the step when the dove landed right beside her. The dove began to take off and do flips in the air. Victoria began to smile. The dove then flew to the vegetable garden. Victoria ran behind the dove until she caught up. Laying inside the scarecrow's pocket was a piece of paper. On one side of the note there was a huge "T" and on the other side was a note. It read:

Dear Victoria,

You are beautiful!

I love it when you smile!

You make My heart smile!

I know you miss your home and friends, but I have a very special purpose for you and your familiy being here. Instead of thinking of all the things you do not have - which will only make you feel sad and gloomy - I want you to focus on all the things you do have.

I made you with a heart that was made to be thankful. I want you to skip around this vegetable garden and begin to tell Me all the things you are thankful for in your life. You will begin to feel the heavy clouds in your heart turn into beautiful rays of sunshine.

I love you!

Father God

Victoria began to skip around the garden. She began to think of all the things she was thankful for. She burst into laughter, and out loud began to thank God for each person and blessing He had brought into her life.

Give thanks no matter what happens.
God wants you to thank him because
you believe in Christ Jesus.
– I Thessalonians 5:18 NIV

She skipped to the front of the house where all of her friends were holding their own pieces of paper. None of them knew where the others had been or what their notes had said. The dove suddenly appeared and took each letter to form a word:

All of a sudden the papers turned into kites and attached to each other. Caleb, Isabella, Samuel and Victoria began floating higher and higher into the sky.

Love – Identity – Forgiveness – Thankfulness

The four truths
God had given them
would raise them up each and every
time difficult circumstances
and people came their way on their
life's journey.

Where there was once fear, sadness, and anger … there was now hope. Fear was replaced with peace, sadness was replaced with joy, and anger was replaced with love.

Your ancestors have also been taught "Love your neighbors and hate the one who hates you." However, I say to you, love your enemy, bless the one who curses you, do something wonderful for the one who hates you, and respond to the very ones who persecute you by praying for them. For that will reveal your identity as children of your heavenly Father.
— Matthew 5:43-44 TPT

Love

1. Like Caleb, has anyone made fun of something that was important to you?

2. Do you understand how much Father God loves you? His love for you does not increase or decrease based on what you do or don't do.

3. Do you believe Father God created you just the way you are?

4. How do you worship God? Do you understand that as long as you worship Him with all of your heart Father God accepts and loves your worship?

5. Who do you believe Father God wants you to love that perhaps you have not been loving?

6. Do you understand that if people knew how much Father God loved them they would not hurt others?

Application Sing 'Jesus Loves Me" and, like Caleb was told, believe the words in your heart.

So now I live with the confidence that there is nothing in the universe with the power to separate us from God's love. – Romans 8:38-39 TPT

Identity

1. Is there something about you that you do not like? For example, Isabella did not like her hair and the color of her clothes.

2. Do you believe Father God made you to be you and no one else?

3. Do you understand that because you are a child of God that makes you a princess or a prince?

4. Is there anyone that affects you in a negative way?

5. Do you understand that when you receive the truth of who you are in Father God's eyes people will stop affecting you the way they have in the past?

6. Do you understand Father God will always accept you and love you for who you are?

Application Look in the mirror and repeat: "I am beautiful (or handsome) in my Father's eyes! I am a Princess (or Prince) and I am treasured by the One who made me!"

Before I formed you in your mother's body, I chose you. Before you were born I set you apart to serve me. I appointed you to be a prophet to the nations.
– Jeremiah 1:5 NIV

Forgiveness

1. Like Samuel, is there anyone who you focus on because they have hurt you?

2. Do you understand Jesus experienced bullying when He was walking on this earth?

3. Do you understand that we must forgive others because that is what Jesus did for us?

4. Do you believe our hearts were not made to hold unforgiveness in it? It will truly turn us into people God never intended us to be.

Application Take a lock with a key and as you unlock the lock repeat these words:
"I forgive _____ (whoever comes to your heart to forgive) for hurting me. I place them into my Father's hands and I bless them in Jesus' name."

Put up with one another. Forgive one another if you are holding something against someone. Forgive, just as the Lord forgave you. – Colossians 3:13 NIRV

Thankfulness

1. Like Victoria, is there something that you are sad about today?

2. Is there something you miss or wish you had today?

3. Do you feel alone and feel no one understands what you are going through?

4. Do you understand Father God loves to see you smile? He smiles when you smile.

5. Do you understand Father God has a very special purpose for you?

6. Do you understand when you focus on all the things you do not have it will make you feel gloomy and sad?

7. Do you understand Father God desires for you to focus on all the things you do have? This will make your heart full of joy.

Application In your imagination skip around in your special place and begin to say aloud all the things and people you are thankful for. You will see the heavy clouds turn into beautiful sunshine.

Give thanks no matter what happens. God wants you to thank him because you believe in Christ Jesus.
– I Thessalonians 5:18 NIV